For my fellow scaredy-cats—and our heroes

Henry Holt and Company, LLC
Publishers since 1866
175 Fifth Avenue, New York, New York 10010
mackids.com

Henry Holt® is a registered trademark of Henry Holt and Company, LLC.
Copyright © 2016 by Mike Curato
All rights reserved.

Library of Congress Cataloging-in-Publication Data is available.
ISBN 978-0-8050-9827-3

Our books may be purchased in bulk for promotional, educational, or business use.
Please contact your local bookseller or the Macmillan Corporate and Premium Sales Department
at (800) 221-7945 ext. 5442 or by e-mail at MacmillanSpecialMarkets@macmillan.com.

First Edition—2016
The artist used pencil on paper and digital color in Adobe Photoshop to create the illustrations for this book.
Printed in China by RR Donnelley Asia Printing Solutions Ltd., Dongguan City, Guangdong Province

1   3   5   7   9   10   8   6   4   2

Little Elliot

BIG FUN

Story and pictures by

MIKE CURATO

Henry Holt and Company • New York

*L*ittle Elliot and his best friend, Mouse, were heading to the far edge of the big city.

205TH ST.

STILLWEL

D | CON

"You will love the boardwalk!" said Mouse.
"I go every year with my family."

"Will there be treats?" asked Elliot.

"Oh yes," said Mouse. "Ice cream and cotton candy and popcorn! And there are shows and games and lots of rides!"

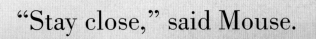

"Stay close," said Mouse.

CHUTES

"Would you like to ride the
water chute?" asked Mouse.

"Too wet," said Elliot.
"What if I fall out of the
boat? I can't swim."

"What about the swings or the giant
roulette wheel?" asked Mouse.

"Too dizzy!" said Elliot.

"How about the roller coaster?" said Mouse. "It's my favorite!"

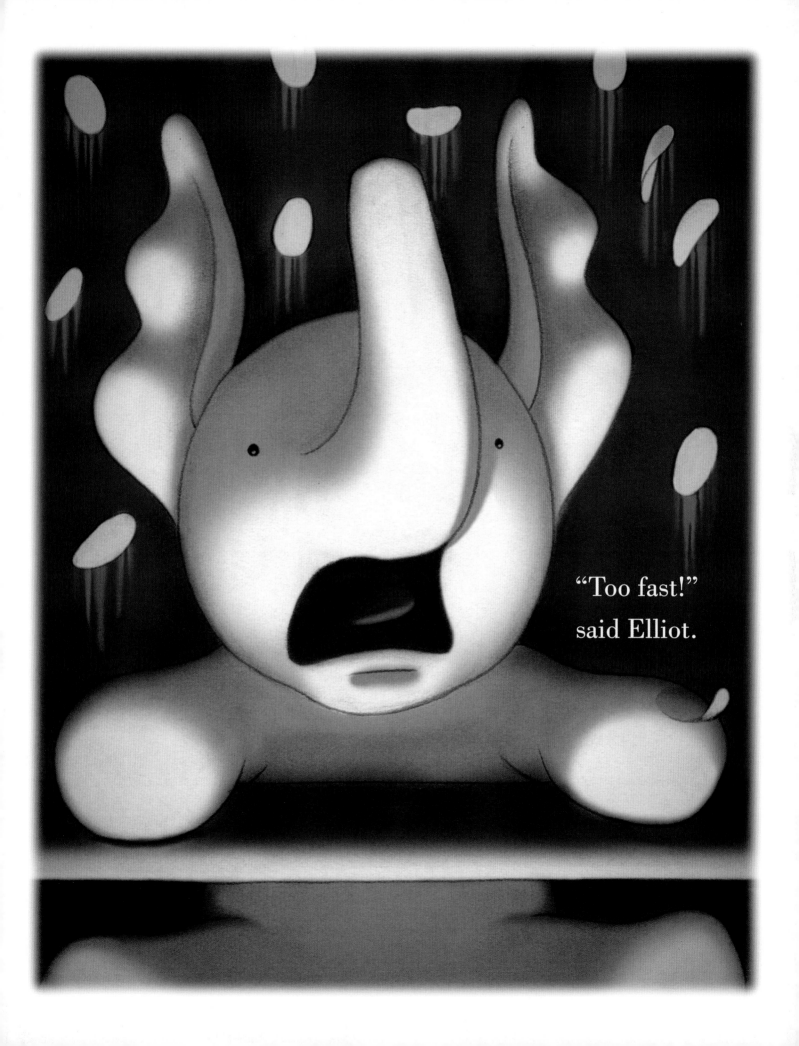

"Too fast!"
said Elliot.

"I think it is time for a treat,"
said Elliot.

"Wait, Elliot!" Mouse shouted.

Elliot was too frightened to stop.

So he ran . . .

. . . and ran

and ran.

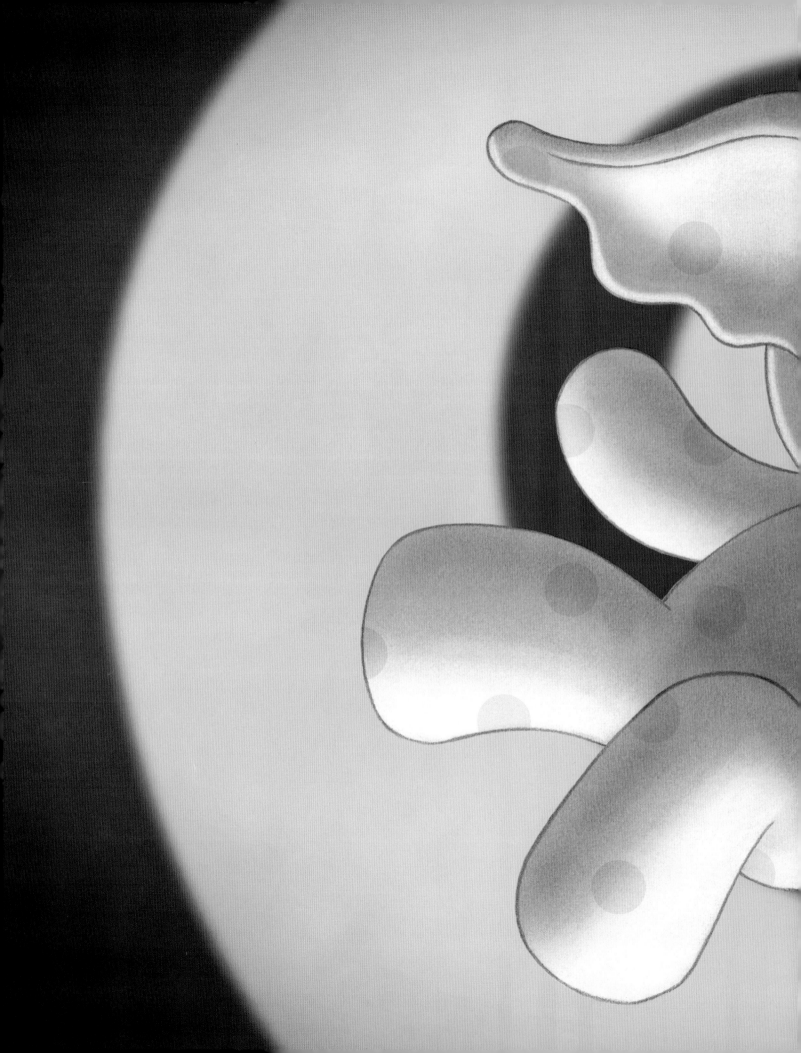

Elliot was NOT having fun.

Elliot couldn't run anymore.
Mouse finally found him.

"Poor Elliot," said Mouse.

"I think it's time for a break."

"Feeling better?" asked Mouse.

"Much better!" said Elliot.
"But I wish there was a ride that
wasn't fast or dizzy or wet."

"I have an idea," said Mouse.

Elliot was nervous,
but Mouse patted his head.

"I'm not so sure about this," said Elliot. "What if it's too windy and we blow away? What if the wheel comes loose and we roll into the ocean? What if SOMETHING HAPPENS?"

"Everything is okay," said Mouse. "I am right here."

Elliot slowly uncovered one eye and peeked out.

"WOW!"
he said.

Finally, Elliot was having fun.
So was Mouse.

"What was your favorite
part of the day?"
asked Elliot.

"Being with you," said Mouse.

"Mine too," said Elliot.

"Being with you is my
favorite part of every day!"